POPPY THE PANDA

FOR LYDIA HERMANSON

Clarion Books
a Houghton Mifflin Company imprint
215 Park Avenue South, New York, NY 10003
Copyright © 1984 by Dick Gackenbach
All rights reserved.
For information about permission to reproduce
selections from this book, write to Permissions,
Houghton Mifflin Company, 2 Park Street, Boston, MA 02108
Printed in the USA

Library of Congress Cataloging in Publication Data

Gackenbach, Dick.
Poppy, the panda.
Summary: Katie can't find the right thing for her
toy panda to wear until her mother comes up with the
perfect solution.
[1. Pandas—Fiction.   2. Toys—Fiction]   I. Title.
PZ7.G117Po 1984   [E]   84-4952
ISBN 0-89919-276-9   PA   ISBN 0-89919-492-3

Printed in the U.S.A.
WOZ 10 9 8

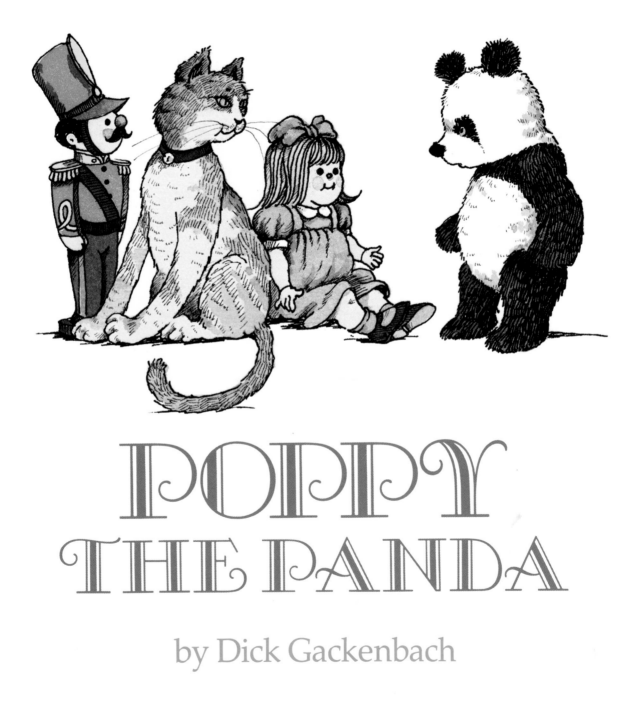

POPPY
THE PANDA

by Dick Gackenbach

CLARION BOOKS / NEW YORK

Katie O'Keefe had a toy panda. His name was Poppy.

Katie took Poppy with her everywhere she went. And Katie would never think about going to bed unless Poppy came, too.

One night Katie told Poppy, "It's time for bed!"

But Poppy refused to go. "I can't sleep when I'm unhappy," he said.

"I didn't know you were unhappy," said Katie.

"Well, I am!" said Poppy. "Everyone has something nice to wear but me. Your doll has a fancy dress. And your soldier has a fine suit and hat. Why, even your cat has a collar. But what do I have to wear?" Poppy complained. "Nothing at all!"

"I'll have to do something about that," said Katie thoughtfully.

"Good," said Poppy. "Otherwise, I doubt if I'll ever want to go to bed."

Katie took the dress off her doll and put it on Poppy.

"There!" she said. "That looks good on you. Now will you come to bed?"

But Poppy would not budge. "I hate it," he said. "I am a boy panda, and I will not wear a dress."

"Fussy, fussy, fussy," said Katie. She looked around her room for something else Poppy could wear. She decided on her roller skates.

"Here," Katie said, putting them on the panda. "Wear these."

Poppy was very shaky on roller skates.
"I-I-I-I'm not sure I approve," he said.
"Skates are fun to wear," Katie told him.
"You'll see." Then she gave Poppy a big
push.

Poppy went forward, weaving and bobbing out of Katie's room and into the hallway. He rolled down the hall to the top of the steps and then over.

BUMPITY, BUMPITY, BUMPITY CLOMP! Poppy went all the way down the steps and landed with a thud at the bottom.

Katie ran down behind him and picked him up. "Are you hurt?" she asked. "I'm so sorry."

She hugged the panda. "Cheer up, Poppy," she said. "We'll find something else for you to wear."

"Please," Poppy said with a sigh. "Something without wheels."

Katie took Poppy to the closet. "Try this on," she said, giving Poppy an umbrella. "Nobody *wears* an umbrella!" he said.

Katie then put two shoes on Poppy.
"They won't do," he said. "They don't
even match."
Katie threw up her arms. "You're so
hard to please, Poppy!"

Katie took Poppy to the dining room.
She put a fruit bowl on his head. Poppy
didn't like that at all.

"I am your best friend," he said. "Not a
banana."

In the kitchen, Katie tried to get Poppy
to wear a saucepan. "It fits fine," she said.
"It's awful!" said Poppy. "People will
laugh at me."

They went upstairs
to the bathroom.
Poppy hated the cape
Katie made from a
towel.

He didn't care for the plastic shower cap, either.

Nor did he like being wrapped in bathroom
tissue. "Where do you get such ideas?" he
asked Katie. "You've made me look like a
package."

They went back to Katie's room. Both
were tired and sleepy, but Poppy still
refused to go to bed.

"Oh, what will I do with you, you silly panda?"

"Just find me something sensible to wear," suggested Poppy. "Is that so difficult?"

Just then, Katie's mother appeared at the bedroom door.

"Katie O'Keefe," she said. "Why aren't you in bed?"

"I'm ready," said Katie. "It's Poppy's fault." She told her mother all about it. "And he's such a fusspot," she said.

"Poor Poppy," said Katie's mother. "If *I* give him something to wear, do you think he'll go to bed?"

"He might," Katie said, "if he likes it."

Katie's mother took the ribbon she was wearing in her hair and tied it in a beautiful bow around Poppy's neck.

"Now, how's that?" she asked.

"It's perfect!" cried Katie. But would Poppy like it? she wondered.

Katie picked Poppy up and held him in front of the mirror so he could see his new ribbon.

While Katie's mother turned down the covers, Poppy smiled. "I love my ribbon," he whispered.

"We're *both* ready for bed now," Katie told her mother.

Katie's mother tucked them in, turned out the light, and closed the door.

"I can't wait to show off my ribbon," Poppy said.

"Tomorrow," Katie said. "But now, good night."

"Good night," said Poppy.

And they both went right to sleep.